"A remarkable feat of writing and performing—a rare autobiographical tour de force so lustrous it seems to reinvent the whole solo-acting genre . . . funny, flavorful and brushed with rich imagery and a tangy idiom . . . ripe with texture and language of a scruffy, vibrant world that appalls, enthralls and enriches us almost simultaneously."
—*Los Angeles Times*

"A personal but surprisingly universal story." —*Newsweek*

"A treat from beginning to end." —*The New Yorker*

"Without a chandelier, an angel, or even a costume change, she recreates each character memorably."
—*New York* magazine

"Theater at its most profound is a celebration of life. All by herself Woodard accomplishes this with far greater ease than many plays that fill their stages with seeming multitudes." —Howard Kissel, *New York Daily News*

"Unabashedly ingratiating . . . charismatic." —*Variety*

CHARLAYNE WOODARD, after studying at Chicago's Goodman School of Drama, moved to New York with only $2,000 and a violin. Within two weeks, she landed a role in the Broadway performance of *Hair.* She later won both Tony and Drama Desk nominations for her work in *Ain't Misbehavin'*, and a second Drama Desk nomination for the Manhattan Theatre Club production of *Hang on to the Good Times.* Her credits include numerous roles with the New York Shakespeare Festival, on television's "Roseanne" and "Fresh Prince," and in regional theater. She lives in Los Angeles.

CHARLAYNE WOODARD

PLUME
Published by the Penguin Group
Penguin Books USA Inc., 375 Hudson Street,
New York, New York 10014, U.S.A.
Penguin Books Ltd, 27 Wrights Lane,
London W8 5TZ, England
Penguin Books Australia Ltd, Ringwood,
Victoria, Australia
Penguin Books Canada Ltd, 10 Alcorn Avenue,
Toronto, Ontario, Canada M4V 3B2
Penguin Books (N.Z.) Ltd, 182–190 Wairau Road,
Auckland 10, New Zealand

Penguin Books Ltd, Registered Offices:
Harmondsworth, Middlesex, England

First published by Plume, an imprint of Dutton Signet,
a division of Penguin Books USA Inc.

Pretty Fire
was first performed as a work-in-progress
at the Fountainhead Theatre Company,
Hollywood, California, on October 16, 1992.

Pretty Fire
was produced in New York City by
the Manhattan Theatre Club
on March 26, 1993.

REGISTERED TRADEMARK—MARCA REGISTRADA

ISBN 0-452-27385-4

Printed in the United States of America
Set in Garamond Light
Designed by Leonard Telesca

ACKNOWLEDGMENTS

Many thanks to my husband, Alan Harris, without whom *Pretty Fire* would've been just another good idea that never saw the light of day.

To all my friends, stage managers, designers, and crews, who said "yes," and in many cases worked for free . . . I owe you one.

DEDICATION

To my parents and grandparents, whose strength, wisdom, and love inspired me to cut a new path.

In memory of Esther Sherman, my agent, who fearlessly picked up the ball, and ran with it.

FOREWORD

In the oral traditions of West Africa and the African diaspora, Charlayne Woodard is a modern-day griot. A magnificent storyteller, this smooth lyricist of life's harmonic complexities weaves a tapestry of Spanish moss, mother wit, and tales of family life that speak of dignity, survival, humor, and strength in a world in which beauty, promise, and opportunity walk hand in hand with pain, hostility, and the "pretty fire" of adversity.

In a world encompassing the fecund red clay of the South and the fertile darker soil of the North, she found both harsh reality and grace and learned lessons in life that are universal in their truths. Her story is a rich gumbo redolent with wit and humor, spiced by the trials and epiphany of a young girl's journey into selfhood. *Pretty Fire* is a symphonic poem challenging the reader to listen, feel, and soar in joy, joined as one with Ms. Woodard.

George C. Wolfe

INTRODUCTION

When I was in first grade, my teacher sent a note home to my mother, informing her that unlike the other children, I never brought anything in for show and tell. Instead, she wrote, I kept the class very entertained by telling them all of our family's "business." My mother put an end to that—very quickly!

As I grew older, I honed my verbal skills at family functions, where cousins would compete with aunts and uncles in sharing the events of their lives. Only the cleverest, the most entertaining, and the loudest ever made it to the end of their story.

Friends were always coming up to me, asking me to tell them this story or that. In ninth grade, my friend Gaydell ran up to me in the lunchroom, followed by a group of girls. She said, "Charlayne, tell us the story of when your grandmother was twelve years old and a man slapped her, and she chopped his ear off with a hoe!"

I was indignant. "Gaydell Young, that is not a story, that is the truth! I didn't make that up! What do you mean, 'tell the story'?"

She said, "Well, just tell it anyway."

And, of course, I did. But I didn't get it. To me, stories

were something that you made up. I was simply telling the truth, as I perceived it. What I didn't realize until years later was that I was a part of an oral tradition stretching back centuries, to Africa, where "griots" turned the events of the day into tales often told through poetry and music. In this way, they passed the customs, beliefs, and history of their tribes on to subsequent generations.

Our oral tradition continued in America when Africans were brought here as slaves, even though their owners prohibited them from speaking their native languages. Before long, the resourceful slaves combined the remnants of their African languages and heritage with words and forms taken from the dominant culture that surrounded them. They created a new language and a new culture, still steeped, of course, in the oral tradition, because the slaves were also prohibited from learning how to read and write.

Growing up, I had no such prohibitions. I was encouraged to be whatever I wanted to be, and I chose to become an actor. My passion was interpreting the words of others, giving them emotional and physical life. I thrived in New York theater.

Then, several years ago, I moved from my culturally diverse, racially integrated world on the Upper West Side of Manhattan to Los Angeles, a culturally diverse but racially segregated city. I found myself associating with either African-American friends or white friends, but rarely both simultaneously.

When my white friends invited me to dinner parties, I often found myself attempting to correct their misconceptions about my people and my culture. Much of what they knew about African-Americans came from the negative images and stereotypes they saw on television and in film. In contrast, we know the white world firsthand because we live in it and must move boldly through it, every single day. We read their books, plays, and newspapers; watch their television shows and movies; attend their art openings; and study their history, philosophies, and religions.

In trying to explain to my friends who we are and where we came from, I truly began to understand who I was and where I came from. As I told them about my childhood and the simple, honest people who raised me, I realized the legacy I had been given.

The experiences I related about the life of an African-American girl on this planet from birth to age eleven were so personal, yet so universal, that we all realized that as different as African-Americans seemed to them, we shared many of the same values, the same fears, and the same dreams.

I was encouraged to write these "stories" of my formative years in the hopes that others might discover these same truths.

The result is *Pretty Fire*, a celebration of my heroes—my parents, my grandparents, and other role models who instilled me with values and courage, and who, with their love, taught me to love.

The personal joy I received from writing the play, and performing it, as well as its success, is, I believe, due to the healing effect it has on audiences at a time when we, as a country and as a world, are torn by racism and brutality.

Charlayne Woodard
Los Angeles, California
April 1994

I came to live out loud.
—Emile Zola

Pretty Fire premiered on October 1, 1992, at the Fountainhead Theatre Company in Hollywood, California.

CAST *Charlayne Woodard*

DIRECTOR *Stuart K. Robinson*
ADDITIONAL DIRECTION *Ken Page*
PRODUCTION DESIGNER *Gregory Van Horn*
PRODUCTION STAGE MANAGER *Christopher Affre*
Produced by *Steven Adams* and *Jacqueline Davis*

This production of *Pretty Fire* subsequently moved to the Odyssey Theatre in Los Angeles, where it opened on November 20, 1992. The only production change was:

Produced by *Frank Gruber* and *Alan M. Harris*

Pretty Fire opened Off-Broadway on March 26, 1993, at The Manhattan Theatre Club's Second Stage, Lynne Meadow, Artistic Director, Barry Grove Managing Director.

CAST *Charlayne Woodard*

DIRECTOR *Pamela Berlin*
SET DESIGN *Shelley Barclay*

COSTUME DESIGNER *Rita Ryack*
LIGHTING DESIGN *Bryan Nason*
SOUND DESIGN *Bruce Ellman*
PRODUCTION STAGE MANAGER *Allison Sommers*

Pretty Fire opened on November 23, 1993, at the Sylvia and Danny Kaye Playhouse in New York City as a Mainstage Production of the Manhattan Theatre Club. Production changes were:

DIRECTOR *Lynne Meadow*
PRODUCTION STAGE MANAGER *Diane DiVita*
PRODUCTION CONSULTANT *Alan M. Harris*

PRETTY
FIRE

Pretty Fire is composed of five stories: "Birth," "Nigger," "Pretty Fire," "Bonesy," and "Joy." There is a single intermission, between "Pretty Fire" and "Bonesy." The stage is bare except for a simple wooden loveseat, light enough for the actor to move easily. It is the only prop the actor uses. All other props are mimed.

BIRTH

"All Blues" by Miles Davis plays. Lights up on CHARLAYNE, *sitting center stage on the loveseat, transported by this music.*

You hear that . . . ?

(Music down.)

It was December twenty-ninth . . . that magical time between the celebration of the birth of Jesus Christ and the celebration of the birth of the brand new year.

It was seven o'clock on a Sunday evening in Albany, New York. A blanket of snow covered the whole town. It had snowed that entire Christmas week. You know, those fat, fluffy snowflakes. The kind that makes you feel like you're in one of those glass snow bubbles that you just shake up. . . . *(She shakes an imaginary snow bubble, then mimes the snow falling all around her.)*

(She moves the loveseat downstage center.)

My parents, Alfred and Dorothy, themselves not yet twenty years old, were relaxing in the living room of their small apartment. They had just spent their first Christmas together as husband and wife. A small Christmas tree stood in the corner, slightly underdecorated—actually *very* under-decorated—with only a few bulbs and ornaments.

My mother . . . *(She crosses to the loveseat and sits.)* She sat in an easy chair next to the window, watching the snow fall, and she was crocheting a tiny white sweater for her first-born, due in eight more weeks. She chose white because she didn't know whether the baby would be a boy or a girl, these being those prehistoric days *before* amniocentesis.

My father . . . *(She shifts to a reclining position on the loveseat; "All Blues" up.)* He was doing his "Sunday thing," on the couch, listening to the hi-fi as his beloved Miles Davis painted pictures with his horn. *(She mimics her father smoking, grooving to the music.)* "Yeah . . . all right . . . ah, look out! Look out! Look out!"

(Music down.)

"All Blues" in the middle of a snowstorm was all right with Daddy.

Suddenly *(music out)* my mother felt a very hot, tingly sensation all through her body. This was accompanied by a very major urge . . . to pee. So she put down her needles and her yarn and *(standing and making her way down an imaginary hallway)* quickly walked down the hallway that led to the bathroom.

"Aooh!" A terrible pain gripped her body. Then, suddenly, with no warning at all, water gushed down her legs and all over the floor. Holding on to the wall for support, my mother walked to the bathroom. She sat down on the toilet. *(Arriving back at the loveseat and sitting, she is racked by another sharp pain.)* "Aaach!"

Instinctively—to this day she doesn't know what made her do it, but my mother just *(reaching one hand under her dress)* put her hand between her legs. . . . *(She withdraws her cupped hand.)*

(Awestruck:) She caught me. She caught . . . me! Just before I would've hit the water in the toilet. My mother took in a deep breath to call for help, but she couldn't, so she swallowed that one and tried another. This time:

"WOODY!!!!!!!!!!"

("All Blues" up.)
(She shifts to Daddy's reclining position on the loveseat.)

"Aw, come on, Dot. Can't I have one day, just one day, when I can kick back and listen to my music?" *(He stands; music out.)*

Reluctant, but obedient to the wishes of his pregnant wife, my father walked down that very same hallway *(walking down the imaginary hallway, slipping on the wet floor)*, slipping and sliding. . . .

"What is this mess, Dot? I suppose you want *me* to clean it up!?"

(He listens.)

Getting no answer, he walked to the bathroom door. He saw us there, my mother, crouched down on the bathroom tiles, holding *me* in the palm of her hand. I was black. Blue-black . . . and fuzzy all over, still attached by the umbilical cord. And looking closer, he could see that my fingers were still slightly webbed.

My father looked into my mother's eyes and saw his own panic staring back at him. Not a word was said.

Daddy ran to the bedroom. He ripped the blanket off the bed. He came back and gently wrapped us in this blanket. Then he found his car keys and he raced outside. It was deserted. Silent. My father's bare feet made the only footprints in that snow. Slipping, sliding, running, falling, he got into the car to turn it on to warm it up. Then he ran back inside. He found his boots, put on his heavy overcoat, found Mommy's pocketbook with all the important papers in it. Finally, he carefully picked us up, carried us down the front steps of 97 Second Street, put us into that car, and my father drove through my snow-covered town at Godspeed.

When Daddy got to the emergency room of Albany Medical Center Hospital, he came running in, holding *us* in his arms. *(Running back and forth across the stage:)* "My wife is having a baby! My wife is having a baby!"

A very officious nurse came from out of nowhere. She said *(with a West Indian accent)*, "Young man, this is a hospital! You can't come screaming in here like that. There are lots of women having babies in this place tonight. Your wife is no different than anybody else."

With that, my father placed us on the nearest chair. He opened up that blanket. The nurse saw me there in the palm of my mother's hand, blue-black, fuzzy, still attached by the umbilical cord. . . .

She took in the same breath that my mother took in, only she said *(screaming)*: "Aaaaaaaaaaaaaaaaaaaahhhh!"

Doctors, nurses, orderlies came from everywhere to help. My father was scooted off in one direction and Mommy and I were scooped up and whisked away in another direction, as they went about the business of trying to save our lives.

In the waiting room, Daddy called his parents, Alfred Sr. and Leola, who lived in the country, five miles outside of Albany. *(On the phone, panicked:)* "Mama! Mama, I'm at the hospital! Come quickly, Mama! The baby is already here."

(As Grandmama, in happy anticipation, with a soft-spoken, rural southern accent:) "What is it, Junior? How much it weigh . . . ?"

"Mama, please! The baby is already here."

(He hangs up.)

My grandmother got dressed and went to the hospital. My grandfather put on his warm clothes and went out into that snowstorm, and he slaughtered a pig. . . .

Oh yes! He knew that family and friends from all over would be coming to celebrate his eldest son's firstborn.

As my father chained-smoked Camels, the news of my birth spread throughout the family. "The baby is here! The baby is here!"

And the Woodard clan fell on that hospital like the snow fell on the ground. My aunts and uncles assaulted my father with a million questions, only Daddy had no answers. So they waited. . . .

They waited for hours. Finally, my mother's doctor walked into that crowded waiting room. He said *(very seriously)*, "The baby is a girl. She weighs one pound, eight ounces. . . . We don't expect her to live through the night. I'm sorry. . . . But your wife is doing fine, Mr. Woodard. She should be able to go home in about a week. She's sedated right now, but you can go in and see her if you like. . . . Uh, one at a time, please."

When my grandmother finally went home, early the next morning, she told Granddaddy this terrible news.

He said *(rural southern accent)*, "Mama, make me an appointment to see the doctor at the same time that I see that baby."

My grandfather found his way to the pediatrics intensive

care unit. There he met up with the doctor and together they approached the glass window that separated me from the rest of the world. *(Palms on the window:)* He saw me lying there, in an incubator, naked, hooked up to tubes everywhere—IV, respirator, heart monitor. . . . No body to speak of, no face even. Just two great big eyes peering out at him. "A pound and a half and lucky to be two days old."

If any of this shocked my grandfather, he certainly didn't show it. He just stood there and poured every ounce of his energy out to that little baby. While doing this, he could faintly hear the doctor going on and on in the background about how unfortunate it is . . . how they've done all they could. . . .

My grandfather cut this man off in mid-sentence. He said, "Excuse me, sir, but we have not called on . . . the Big Man yet! Where is your chapel?"

The doctor directed Granddaddy down the hall. He entered that empty chapel and approached the altar. *(Kneeling and humming as he enters the presence of his God:)* "Yes . . . yes . . . yes . . . yes . . . yes . . . yes. . . . Oh Lord, I come before you, your humble servant. I come acknowledging that you are my God—my King—my Father. And I am your child. That's why, Lord, I know I can come boldly before your throne and ask you right now, Lord, heal my li'l grandchild. Right the wrong. Breathe air into her little lungs. Make her heart beat strong. In the name of Jesus! Lord, make her an example to the whole world, of your miracle-working power. Hallelujah! I know you're able. . . . I thank you, Lord. I thank you already. . . . Amen."

(Standing:) With that my grandfather rose to his feet, triumphant, secure in the knowledge that now I was in God's hand.

Several days later, he and my grandmother returned to the

hospital to visit with my mother, who had regained her strength. He said, "Well, now, Dot, what you gonna name the child?"

(Proudly:) "Well . . . Woody and I were thinking of naming her . . . Africa."

(Outraged:) "Africa?! How you gonna name the child Africa, Dot? She's gonna have a hard enough time of it as it is. Look at her! She's a girl, she's underdeveloped, she's blue-black! Africa! People gonna think she jumped out of somebody's Tarzan movie. You can't name her Africa, Dot! She's a child, not a land mass!"

My mother took this into consideration and came up with a second choice. "Okay, then—what about . . . Charlayne?" After her favorite uncle, Charlie. "And Elizabeth," after her own middle name. And, of course, Woodard.

Granddaddy rolled that one around on his tongue. "Charlayne Elizabeth Woodard. . . . Whooie, Dot! That is a mighty big name for such a lee li'l girl!"

But my mother held her ground this time. She said, "Well . . . she'll just have to grow into it."

And I tried.

With each passing week, the doctors said I wouldn't make it through the next. That I might be blind. I might be deaf. I might have brain damage. They didn't know for sure, but I certainly wouldn't be a normal child!

All this time my father believed everything those doctors said, and he never once came to see me while I was in the hospital. Now that's not to say Daddy didn't love me. No, it was quite the opposite. You see, he was afraid of getting attached to someone born too soon and destined to die too soon.

Granddaddy, on the other hand, knew that sooner or later, that baby was coming home. He approached my parents.

"Dot, Junior, when that baby gets out of the hospital, ya'll gonna have to move on out to the country. Let Mama help you with that child, because ya'll don't know nothing about no babies, premature or otherwise."

And Granddaddy, who had frozen that pig he slaughtered back on December twenty-ninth, started chopping wood for the furnace that heated that big old farmhouse. *(Chopping wood:)* "Yeah . . . this drafty old house gonna have to be kept warm 'cause that baby is not gonna get sick, no sir, not in my house, no sir, not on my account!" *(Stops chopping.)*

Weeks turned into months. The seasons changed. Finally, eleven months after I was born, I came home to Granddaddy's house. When I arrived, three surprises greeted me.

The first surprise was from my grandfather. The wood that he had chopped was stacked the length of the barn and went all the way to the roof!

The second surprise was from my mother—a two-week-old *baby sister*, weighing in at eight pounds at birth. Her name was Allie. She had arrived at Granddaddy's house just one week before me . . . their little insurance policy in case I didn't make it.

("All Blues" up. She hears the music.)

And my third surprise? *(Searching to see:)* . . . Daddy . . . ? *(Recognizing him:)* Daddy!

(She reaches for him.)

Blackout.

NIGGER

"ABC Song" plays. Lights up on CHARLAYNE *as she mimes jumping rope across the stage, singing along with the music.*

". . . H-I-J-K-L-M-MINTO-P!"

(Boasting:) I learned my ABC's in one night! Thanks to my Aunt Ruby, who gave me a big, beautifully illustrated ABC book, and thanks to my father, who taught them to me.

One night, after dinner, Daddy said, "Charlayne, go get me that big pretty ABC book and meet me on the couch." *(Moving loveseat stage left:)* I did this. *(Sitting on the loveseat:)* I sat next to Daddy and he opened that big pretty book on both of our laps.

He said "This is an A. This is a B. This is a C. This is a D. What is this, Charlayne?"

"Q?"

(Daddy slaps her on the back of her hand. She's shocked.)

"This is an A. This is a B. This is a C. This is a D. What is this, Charlayne?"

"B?"

(Slaps her hand.)

"This is an A, this is a B, this is a C, this is a D. Pay attention, Charlayne. What is this, Charlayne?"
"A?"
"Very good, Charlayne. And what is this?"
"B?"
"Very good, Charlayne. And what is this?"
"D?"

(Slaps her hand, then more slaps for emphasis.)

This . . . went . . . on . . . all . . . night . . . long . . . until sunrise, when finally I could identify every letter of the alphabet, backwards, forwards, and out of sequence.

Mommy was mortified, but Daddy was determined. My sister, Allie, had watched as much she could from underneath the coffee table in front of us. Then she fell asleep and Mommy put her to bed late that night.

The next morning at breakfast, Daddy said, "Allie, tonight *you're* gonna learn *your* ABC's."

I teased her, I taunted her all day long. *(Singsong:)* "Allie's gonna learn her ABC's tonight! Allie's gonna learn her ABC's tonight!"

Allie tried desperately to be brave. She said *(feigning glee)*, "Hip, hip hooray! Hip, hip hooray!"

That evening at dinner Allie hardly ate a thing. I wonder why. . . .

After dinner, Daddy said, "Allie, go get that big, pretty ABC book and meet me on the couch."

Allie took my place, right next to Daddy on the couch *(sitting on loveseat)* and I took her place right up under that coffee table.

Daddy opened that big, pretty book on both of their laps. "This is an A, this is a B, this is a C, this is a D. What is this, Allie?"

(Allie laughs nervously, then blurts out:)

"L-M-MINTO-P?!"

(He slaps her hand.)

My sister wailed! My sister screamed! My sister wept crocodile tears! Then, she started peeing on the couch.

(Standing:) "Get her off my couch, Woody!" Mommy screamed. "Get her off my couch!"

Then Allie peed all over the living-room rug.

Oooh! Mommy was furious . . . but not with Allie. Oh no. "See what you did, Woody?! This is all *your* fault. You know . . . you know you can't put Allie under any pressure! *(To Allie:)* Mama's little baby . . . Come on, Allie . . . let Mama clean you up. Yes, yes . . . It's all over, Allie. *(She glares at Daddy.)* It's all over.

(Pause.)

So . . . when I entered kindergarten, I could already read. My sister Allie can't read to this day!

Just kidding!

But as a result of my reading ability, at the beginning of third grade, I was placed into an accelerated program. It was called the "AT." We were "academically talented!"

So on the first day of school, instead of Mommy walking me and Allie up Second Street to School 6, she and Allie walked me *down* Second Street to the bus stop, where I'd catch the bus that was to take me all the way across town to my new school—School 20.

At the bus stop my mother gave me a pep talk—of sorts. She said, "Charlayne, your job is to be smart. Your job is to do your schoolwork, do whatever your teacher tells you to do, and do it well. Now, the other kids in your class will probably have a lot of help from their parents, from their older sisters and brothers. You won't have any help. Your parents are working so hard to take care of this family, we are working round the clock to pay the bills, to give you and Allie a comfortable life. But you've got the right stuff to do this on your own, otherwise they wouldn't have chosen you. Yes?"

(Thinking:) "I'm gonna do it, Mommy!"

The bus came and my mother kissed me on my forehead. I boarded that bus *(sitting on the loveseat, which is now the bus)* and I waved to them. I waved to them until I couldn't see them anymore. I tell you, this "right stuff" was turning out to be a double-edged sword. While I was ready for the challenge, here I was being taken away from everything I knew and loved: my neighborhood, my friends, my school, and most of all, my Allie.

Oh, but the difference between School 6 and School 20 was like night and day.

First of all, there were only sixteen kids in my classroom! And they said it would stay this way until seventh grade. Second of all, Randy French and I were the only two *negro* kids in the whole school. But I looked forward to making new friends. And I did! Barbara O'Dooley, Linda Fraley, and myself, we were inseparable.

I loved my teacher, Mrs. Rosenblatt. I loved all the work she gave me, and I put all my books and papers in a big red-plaid book bag that Daddy'd bought me for the first day of school.

Oh . . . ! One day at recess, some classmates and I were about to race across the schoolyard.

Mrs. Rosenblatt stood way up at the finish line, with her arms outstretched. She yelled, "Get on your mark . . ."

*(*CHARLAYNE *gets into a starting position.)*

"Get set . . ."

Then I heard another voice ring out. *(Singsong:)* "Run, nigger, run!"

*(*CHARLAYNE *stands and looks around.)*

Again Mrs. Rosenblatt called out, "Get on your mark . . ."

*(*CHARLAYNE *gets into a starting position.)*

"Get set . . ."

(Singsong:) "Run, nigger, run."

(She stands again and looks out into the audience.)

This time I recognized the voice. It was Barbara O'Dooley. . . . Mrs. Rosenblatt yelled, "Charlayne, you've got to get on your mark!"

And I told her, "I'm not running!"

Then Barbara yells out so everyone can hear, "Why not? My father said that all niggers can run fast!"

Well, Mrs. Rosenblatt did the running that day! She raced across that schoolyard, grabbed Barbara O'Dooley by the arm, and marched her up those stairs and into that classroom.

No one had ever called me that name before! It felt as if somebody had come up behind me and punched me in my back. The other kids thought it was very funny. They were all laughing. It felt as if they were all calling me. . . .

That day, for the first time since school started, I couldn't wait for that school bus to come and take me away from School 20.

When I got home, my mother was working in the garden out by the peach tree.

(Angry to the point of tears:)

"Mommy! Mommy, they called me a nigger today in school, Mommy! Barbara O'Dooley said, 'Run, nigger, run.' "

My mother put down her tools, took off her gloves, she stood up, and she . . . started laughing! She laughed and she laughed. She couldn't stop laughing!

(Confused:) "Mommy! Please . . . !"

Finally, my mother collected herself. She looked around the yard. "Charlayne, what if I were to call you a . . . rabbit pellet? *(Singsong:)* Run, rabbit pellet, run!"

"No, Mommy! That's not what they said! They called me—"

"Okay, what if I were to call you . . . a stinkweed? Come on over here, stinkweed, and give Mama some sugar!"

"Mommy, please, you're being silly!"

"Yes. I am being silly. But if I'm silly enough to call you a stinkweed, does that make you a stinkweed . . . ? Huh . . . ? Are you a stinkweed?"

*(*CHARLAYNE *takes this in.)*

And then *I* looked around the yard.

(Tentatively:) "You're a peach pit, Mommy!"

"And you're a rabbit pellet!"

(Circling the loveseat, which is now the peach tree, delighted:) "Peach pit!"

"Rabbit pellet!"

"Stinkweed!"

"Froggy face!"

My mother chased me round and round that peach tree as we called each other the most ridiculous names, until finally we just fell out on the grass *(collapsing to the stage)*, exhausted. Then my mother crawled over to me. She said, "Charlayne, 'nigger' is just a word—a word that people purposely made up so they can sling it at us whenever they want to hurt us, whenever they want to *stop* us from doing what we should and being who we are. Now think. Why would Barbara want to hurt you?"

(She thinks.)

"Because I was going to win that race . . . ? Like I always do?"

"Did you win?"

"No, Mommy, I couldn't even run."

"So . . . Barbara beat you today. . . . And all because of that silly word."

(Pause.)

And then I understood.

"Charlayne, if anybody wants to call you a rabbit pellet, you just let them . . . and secretly laugh to yourself: 'How silly *they* are!' Because you know you are not a rabbit pellet, you are not a stinkweed. . . ."

*(*CHARLAYNE *stands with the realization:)* "And, Mommy . . . I am not . . . a nigger."

Blackout.

PRETTY FIRE

Instrumental version of "Dixie" plays. Lights up on CHARLAYNE, *sitting cross-legged on the loveseat.*

One day, when Allie and I were watching old black-and-white movies, Mommy walked into the living room and turned off the TV. She said, "Ladies, tell me, what would you like to *be* when you grow up?"

(Raising her hand:) "Me first, Mommy, me first! *(Standing:)* I want to be . . . Lassie. Yes, Mommy, I want to run through the field and jump over the fence, and see . . . the little girl . . . trapped in the mine . . . and I will call for help! *(Barking:)* Arf, arf, arf, arf, arf, arf, arf, arf, arf, arf! And everyone will come and they will save that little girl trapped in the mine. Then they'll say, 'Good girl, Lassie. *(Reacting to her neck being petted, as if she's a dog:)* Good girl, Lassie. . . .' And Mommy, they will love me!"

My mother said, "Now, now, Charlayne. You don't have to be a *dog* to get love in this family."

(CHARLAYNE, *barking:)* "Arf! Arf! Arf!—"

(Her mother warns:) "That's enough of that!"

"Arf, arf, arf!"

"I done told you—"

"Arf, arf, arf, arf!"

(Losing it:) "Sit your butt down . . . ! *(Collecting herself:)* Okay . . . now, ladies, tell me . . . what kind of . . . *human being* would you like to be when you grow up?"

*(*CHARLAYNE *sits and raises her hand.)*

"Second chance, Mommy! Please, second chance! *(She stands.)* I want to be . . . Shirley Temple. Yes, Mommy . . . I *need* to be Shirley Temple! Oh, Mommy, I want to live in a big white marble house with a huge spiral staircase that goes all the way up to heaven! And I will stand at the top of this staircase, right next to my happy negro butler! All dressed up in tux and tails and clean white gloves! And together we will come tap-dancing down that staircase . . . *(Tap-dancing downstage:)* Shabalabala! Shabalabala! *(Singing and tap-dancing:)*

"I wish I was in the land of cotton,
Old times there are not forgotten,
Look away, look away, look away, Dixieland."

(She finishes with a flourish and freezes in a minstrel pose.)

"Aaah!"

(Pause.)

Then Allie broke in *(raising her hand):* "My turn, Mommy! Please! My turn!"

And Mommy said, "Very good, Allie. Your turn is next. Charlayne . . . sit down!"

And Allie said, "Mommy, I want to be the happy negro maid, Mommy! Oh, Mommy! I want to be in charge of everything! Especially the big, wonderful kitchen, Mommy, with the six-foot-long freezer like Granddaddy's, and I will thaw out all the turkeys and all the hams, and I will bake them up and serve them out on the veranda to . . . *(serving an audience member)* the Colonel . . . and . . . *(serving* CHARLAYNE *on the loveseat)* to my sister . . . Shirley Temple! *(Singing and tap-dancing:)*

"In Dixieland I'll take my stand,
To live and die—"

(Mother, clapping her hands, irritated:) "That's enough! That's enough of this Dixie stuff! You cannot be Lassie, you cannot be Shirley Temple, and you *will not* be a maid! Now I want you both to go on outside and *meditate* on what I just said! Go on! Go on and play! *(She shoos them out, watches them play, then stamps her foot for emphasis.)* Stop that barking!"

Allie and I ran out into the back of the backyard, way out by the peach tree where Mommy couldn't hear us, and we sang "Dixie" . . . sotto voce *(singing sotto voce, in a blues style, with a stylized cakewalk:)*

"In Dixieland, I'll take my stand,
To live and die in Dixie."

(Pause.)

Oh, we loved "Dixie" . . . because "Dixie" meant the South. And the South meant our grandparents—Mommy's parents—Grace Harris and Joe Harris. They lived in Dixie.

As a matter of fact, in my neighborhood, everybody's grandparents lived in Dixie! When summertime came, nobody cared about which camp you were going to. Day camp . . . overnight camp . . . please! The subject never even came up. As far as we were concerned, we were all going down to Dixie, where our grandparents spoiled us silly! As far as we were concerned, Dixie meant *Freedom*!

On the day of departure, Daddy would pull that big black Ford round to the front of the house and load up the trunk with our suitcases. He and Mommy had the front seat *(she sits on the loveseat)*, Allie and I would be in the back. We each had a window!

And we were off!

Now, Allie and I knew we were truly in Dixie when we saw . . . the *lace* trees. *(To an audience member:)* You know what a lace tree is? . . . No? *(She stands.)* It has a huge, brown trunk with great wide branches holding thousands and thousands of leaves. And draped from each branch is this beautiful, flowing gray lace. Of course, Mommy called it—*moss.* But we knew better. These were the lace trees. *(Becoming flowing, seductive, and southern:)* "Welcome to Dixie. I am your lace tree, here to shield you from the hot southern sun. Yes ma'am! You in Dixie now!" *(Singing and doing a patty-cake with Allie:)*

> "In Dixieland I'll take my stand,
> To live and die in Dixie!"

Next stop—3906 Fifth Street, Savannah, Georgia, Rosignol Hill. That's where my grandparents lived. Rosignol Hill—twenty miles outside of Savannah. Rosignol Hill—only *black* people lived here! My grandparents lived up near the top of Rosignol Hill, and my grandmother, Grace Harris, looked down her nose at anyone living . . . *in the bottom.*

Daddy would drive that black Ford over those red clay roads and pull up right in front of Grandmama's yard.

Grandmama and Granddaddy would be up on the front porch, waving and throwing kisses. . . .

Allie and I'd rip ourselves out of that car and they would come down those stairs and smother us with hugs and kisses and I just knew . . . this was gonna be a summer of love!

My parents only stayed in Dixie for one week, because there was this man in Dixie that my mother didn't like. *(Troubled, angry:)* "I tell you, Woody, I can't take this. I'm not used to this anymore. I tell you, I just can't stand Jim Crow!"

(Pause.)

So after a week, Daddy drove Mommy back to Albany. Then we had our grandparents all to ourselves, for the whole summer.

I tell you, everything was *different* in Dixie! People had different jobs in Dixie. Wonderful jobs. Outdoor jobs. Jobs like . . . picking beans and picking corn and picking cotton. Yes!

And if you didn't want to pick your own food, the food came to you. There was this man who drove a big green truck all over Rosignol Hill. *(Miming driving, singing out:)* "Okra! Pecans! Watermelon! Okra! Pecans! Watermelon!"

Then, there was this lee, little man who wore a big straw hat that fell over his eyes. He came pushing a heavy cart. *(She mimes pushing cart along.)*

"Crabs, lobster, swimps! I got your swimps here! Crabs, lobster, swimps! I got your swimps here!"

All of a sudden, in the middle of a bright, sunny day, the whole sky would just open up and buckets and buckets of rain would pour down on us . . . while the sun was still shining. My grandmother would let us play in this rain . . .

barefoot! And that red clay road in front of Grandmama's house turned into red clay mud. *(To an audience member:)* Do you know what it feels like to have some red clay mud squishing in between your toes?

Heaven!

Allie and I would play in this mud, and we would get filthy, filthy, filthy dirty, because you can get dirty in Dixie!

That's because every single night we took a bath. Right before dark, Allie and I would take a bucket out to the front yard. See, my grandmother had no running water in her house, so we'd fill this bucket up at the hydrant. Then Allie would take one half of the handle and I'd take the other and we'd carry it in to Grandmama, who was in the kitchen. She poured the water into a big pot of water she had heating on the stove. Allie and I would make four or five trips back and forth, back and forth, until that pot was full.

Then Grandmama would take a big tub into the dining room—same tub she had washed clothes in earlier that day in the backyard—same tub folks in Chicago barbecue in. And she'd pour all that warm water into this tub. Then she'd take a cake of soap, get down on one knee, and *(kneeling at the tub)* she'd "sudsy up that water and sudsy up that water" until there was a mountain of white, fluffy bubbles. *(Standing:)* Finally, she'd *(opening a tiny jar and pouring)* pour in a little bit of *sweetness* . . . smelled like coconuts!

Allie and I would strip naked right there in the dining room, take off those filthy clay clothes, and *together* we would *(stepping in)* step into this tub of warm, sudsy water . . . that smelled just like Grandmama.

My grandmother would scrub us clean. When we stood up, we had white bubbles and suds sticking all over our bodies. So Grandmama would take a dipper and dip it into a bucket of clear, clean, warm water standing near, and then she would *(pouring water over her head)* pour this water all over our bodies. And this would be our shower. *(She steps out of tub.)* Then she'd wrap us up in a huge towel and pat us dry, all over. *(Patting herself and humming "Dixie".)* Then, we'd put on our pajamas and it was dinnertime!

I tell you, my grandmother was our hero! She was afraid of nothing! She would sit us on the front porch *(moves love-seat center stage)* and teach us "life lessons."

(She becomes Grace Harris, a tall, dignified woman with a strong voice. She paces back and forth across the porch.)

"Never let anybody have the last word if you know you right! Okay, repeat after me. Never let anybody have the last word—"

"Grandmama, I don't understand."

"Okay . . . *(She thinks.)* I recall a time when Miss Minnie Gowire, down there in that bottom, was throwing a big, fancy wedding for her oldest daughter, Pearlene. Well, I went across the highway to the shopping center and I bought Pearlene a nice gift. I came back and wrapped it up pretty my own self. I got dressed and I went on down there in that bottom to the wedding. I enjoyed myself at the wedding, ate myself silly at the reception. . . . When I'd had enough, I came on back up the hill. Now, here I am, sitting on my *own* front porch, minding my own business, when I looked down in that bottom and I noticed a commotion going on down at Minnie Gowire's house. Next thing I see, Miss Minnie Gowire come flyin' out of her house, come sailin' up the road, had her daughters trailin' behind her. Next thing I know, Miss Minnie Gowire came right up and planted herself *condaptly* in my front yard, placing her hands on her hips, and said, 'Grace Harris, how you gonna work a root on my daughter?'

" 'Minnie Gowire, what you talking about?'

" 'You gave my child used sheets! And if she ever tries to *conceive* on those used sheets, she will lose her baby!'

" 'Minnie Gowire, please! I went 'cross to Perdee's department store my own self, and I *bought* Pearlene two sets of sheets for her bed. I came home, wrapped 'em up pretty my own self, brought 'em down there, and placed them condaptly on the dining-room table alongside everybody else's gift. What I wanna work a root on Pearlene for anyhow? I'm glad she's finally getting married . . . old as she is!'

"At that time, Minnie Gowire made a big mistake. 'Cause Miss Minnie Gowire stepped up onto my front porch, and she . . . she put her finger in my face. At that time, I grabbed Minnie Gowire by the scruff of her neck and the seat of her drawers. At that time, I raised Minnie Gowire up over my head, and I *dashed* Minnie Gowire across the side of my porch! That time, Minnie Gowire sailed through the air, she *skeet the pee like a polecat*! At that time, Minnie Gowire hit the ground. *(Stamping her foot:)* Bam! Her children went to collect up they mama, take her on back down in that bottom where she belonged!

"When Minnie got halfway between my house and her place in that bottom, Minnie Gowire bunked over, like this here—in the middle of the road—threw her dress up over her head. Showed me her natural behind! And said, 'Grace Harris, kiss my ass!'

"I said, 'Minnie Gowire . . . you the one with the neck like a giraffe, kiss your own ass!'

(Pause.)

(To the children:) "Don't you ever let anybody have the last word if you know you right! *(Pause.)* 'Course, all of that was before I was saved, sanctified, and filled with the Holy Ghost! Hallelujah!"

I tell you, my grandmother was our hero! She was afraid of nothing!

One evening, just before dark, just before it was time to get our bathwater, we were all outside playing in the road. Miss Minnie came running up out of the bottom and grabbed her grandchildren, Von and Jimmy, by their arms and marched them back down the hill to her house.

The next thing we knew, parents and grandparents all over Rosignol Hill were grabbing children left and right, and whisking them off into their houses.

"What's the matter? What did we do . . . ? I'm sorry."

Allie and I didn't know what to do, so we just went and stood up under that pecan tree across the road from Grandmama's house. Soon, Grandmama came out on her porch looking for us.

"Over here, Grandmama! We're over here!"

Grandmama ran down those steps, raced across that road, grabbed us both by the arms, pulled us into the house, and *threw* us up against the wall, under the windowsill.

(She falls on the floor, up against the loveseat, leaving room for Allie, who's sitting right next to her.)

"What's the matter, Grandmama? What did we do?"

"Ssssh! Pray!"

"But what are we praying for?"

"Ssssh! I said pray now!"

Granddaddy was seated right in front of us, in his rocking chair, facing the window. He had his glasses on, his Bible open on his lap, and *he* was praying. " 'The Lord is my shepherd, I shall not want. He maketh me to lie down in green pastures, he leadeth me beside the still waters. He restoreth my soul. . . . Yea, though I walk through the valley of the shadow of death, I will fear no evil. . . .' "

Grandmama was sitting just in back of Granddaddy, against the opposite wall, but on the floor, just like us, facing us. We all just sat there as it got darker and darker.

(Lights slowly come down.)

Soon, night replaced the day.

I could just make out my grandmother, *crawling* across the floor. She crawled into the kitchen. I saw the refrigerator light go on; after a moment it went off. Then Grandmama crawled back out of the kitchen, and through the darkness, she handed me and Allie both a pie tin *(reaching for pie tin)* full of cold corn, cold rice, and cold fish. She said, "Eat now."

But we couldn't eat. *(She puts the pie tin aside.)* We just sat there . . . until it was pitch black. . . . *(She sits, frightened, in the dark.)*

And then I heard it:

WHOOOOOOOOOOOSH!

(Excited:) Then we saw them flickering, flickering, in Granddaddy's glasses. Allie and I *had* to turn around! We just had to turn around and . . . peek out that window. *(She turns around, kneeling.)* Only our eyes, only our eyes . . . above that windowsill. . . . And there it was! *(The light of a burning cross fills the room.)* Not two, like in Granddaddy's glasses, but one great big Jesus Christ cross! Flaming! Burning in the black night . . . ! *(Arms outstretched; awestruck; she speaks to the cross.)* "Beautiful . . . ! Pretty fire . . . ! Pretty fire . . . ! *(To Allie, as they applaud softly:)* Pretty fire! *(To the cross:)* Pretty fire!"

Suddenly, my grandmother came from nowhere. She yanked us around and shoved us back up against that wall. *(She falls back to the floor, up against the loveseat.)* She looked right into our faces and said, "That is not *pretty*! That is *ugly*! That is the *ugliest* thing you will ever see!"

(Pause.)

I looked into my grandmother's face . . . filled with fire . . . and for the first time in my life, I saw . . . that Grandmama was afraid.

(Pause.)

She sat there with us all through the night as we watched that cross burn in Granddaddy's eyes. *(She falls asleep.)*

(Lights up, slowly.)

The next morning we woke to the smell of sausages cooking in the kitchen. And we were in our bed. The same bed Mommy slept in when she was a little girl.

(Standing:) Allie and I got dressed and went into the dining room to join Granddaddy and Grandmama for breakfast.

But everything was different this morning. All through breakfast, nobody spoke. Not one word.

(Pause.)

When breakfast was over, Allie and I went out on the front porch and we looked up and down that road. . . . Not a soul was out.

(Pause.)

Granddaddy was watching us through the screen door. Then he said . . . "Who wants to go across to the shopping center and buy a pair of flip-flops?"

Flip-flops?! We loved flip-flops! "Take me, Granddaddy! Take me!"

Granddaddy took us both by the hand and we walked down that red clay road. Down to the bottom, down past Miss Minnie's, to the ditch. You see, there was a big ditch at the bottom of Rosignol Hill. In order to get to the highway you had to *(she climbs)* climb down, down, down *into* this ditch, then climb around on the side of the ditch, making sure not to fall into that stinky brown water in back of us, and then we had to climb up, up, up out of this ditch until we finally made it to the highway. Mommy likes to say they put that ditch there purposely, just to humiliate colored people.

(She giggles at this, then . . . notices the charred cross.)

And there it was. It was . . . big. Oh, it was much bigger than it looked from Grandmama's window. And it was . . . black . . . with charcoals stuck to it all the way to the top. And . . . it had a horrible smell. . . . Grandmama was right. . . . It *was* ugly. . . .

(She sings in a painful, angry dirge, as the light of the burning cross slowly fills the stage:)

"I wish I was in the land of cotton,
Old times there are not forgotten.
Look away, look away, look away, Dixieland."

Blackout.

INTERMISSION

BONESY

The intro to Aretha Franklin's "Respect" plays.

Lights up on CHARLAYNE *upstage center. She sings and dances her way downstage, doing snatches of the Boogaloo, the Four Corners, and the Jerk. Loveseat is stage left.*

When I was ten years old, there was nothing I loved better than . . . a talent show. Every single Saturday, kids from up and down Second Street would come into my backyard and we would rehearse. We knew all the groups, we knew all the moves, we knew all the lyrics by heart. We took these rehearsals very seriously. Oh yes! You never knew who might come driving up Second Street. We could get *discovered* or something!

Later on that afternoon, everyone would return to my house with whatever costumes they could put together from their parents' closets. *(Stepping onto loveseat:)* Only this time, we'd be on my front stoop. *This* would be our *stage*, so that the whole neighborhood could hear us and see us. *I* was the mistress of ceremonies. *I* was the judge. *I* won every single Saturday. What? It was my stoop!

(She jumps down.)

Know what else I loved more than anything back then? I loved . . . a secret. I'd give my eyetooth for anyone to share a secret with me. And kids did! Oh yes. They'd tell me their secrets, and I wouldn't tell a soul. To this day, I have those secrets locked up in my heart.

But *I* had secrets I never told. Secrets I never shared with . . . *(she finds an audience member)* anyone.

(Pause.)

Let's share some secrets this evening. . . . I'll go first.

When I was ten years old, my aunt Carolyn moved up from Savannah to live with us, while she went to nursing school. Every day when Allie and I came home from our schools, my aunt Carolyn would call us into her room. *(Primping in the mirror:)* "Charlayne, Allie! *(As she waits for her nieces, she sings to "Shotgun" by Junior Walker and the All Stars and does the Soulfinger. The girls interrupt her.)* Do me a favor and run up to Bernie's corner store. Get me a block of Philadelphia cream cheese and a bag of onion and garlic potato chips. Here, honey. *(She takes a dollar from her bosom.)* Hurry back before your momma and your daddy get home."

Now, in order to get to Bernie's corner store, Allie and I had to walk up Second Street, past School 6, past some neat little houses that looked a lot like ours. . . . It was a nice walk . . . until we reached that last house just before the corner. This house was right out of a horror movie. If it wasn't condemned, it should've been. This is where Robert Blair lived. . . . Robert Blair. And his seven, rude, lowlife, snot-dribbling-out-of-their-noses, bound-for-the-detention-center brothers. If they had parents, nobody knew. We never saw them. Just those Blair boys, out on their stoop, all hours of the day and night, shooting spitballs, cursing, smoking cigarettes. . . .

Allie and I would start up Second Street . . . holding hands. *(She walks across the stage.)* We had our heads bowed to the ground. We were trying to be invisible. "Ssssh! Stop breathing, Allie. They might hear us!"

(Looking up:) Too late. Robert Blair spotted us before we even got near his house. He'd come slithering across his old front yard *(becoming Robert Blair, walking with an obvious "pimp," smoking)*, had a cigarette dangling out the side of his mouth, lean up against his old, raggedy fence.

(Menacing:) "Bonesy! Hey, Bonesy! When you and your liver-lipped sister gonna give me some?"

(Pause.)

And as if that wasn't bad enough, he'd sic his dog, Sooner, on us. "Sick 'em, Sooner! Sic 'em!"

Now, Sooner was the dog from hell. He had one white, blind eye, with a whole lot of white stuff dribbling out of that. Then he had one black eye, that just came at you, like daggers.

Old Sooner'd come tearing down that front stoop. I'd grab Allie's hand and we'd jump up on the nearest parked car. *(She runs and jumps.)* "No, Sooner! No, boy! Please, Sooner! Down! Down, boy! Down! No! Stay, Sooner! Stay. Good boy. . . ."

(She runs to safety.)

Made it to Bernie's!

(She tries to catch her breath.)

"Hi, Bernie. A block of Philadelphia cream cheese and a bag of onion and garlic potato chips, please."

(She hands him the money.)

Bernie would pass us the food over the counter, in a brown paper bag, and hand us our change.

(Pause.)

Now we had to get home. . . . Allie and I would look each other dead in the eye . . .

"Get on your mark, get set, go!"

And we'd tear out of Bernie's, running down Second Street, as fast as we could, but as soon as we passed Robert Blair's house, he'd sic that dog on us *(running in a large circle)*, and old Sooner would be right on our heels, right on our heels. . . . And not until we got past School 6 did Robert Blair call his mangy dog back home. *(She stops running.)*

Then we'd go into our house and give Aunt Carolyn her food and her change. She'd give us both . . . a nickel.

Every single school day, we risked our lives for a block of Philadelphia cream cheese and a bag of onion and garlic potato chips.

Oh, but then came Saturday. We loved Saturday, because Saturday meant no going to school, no going to Sunday school, even. And no going to Bernie's! Because my aunt didn't dare send us on errands when my parents were at home.

On Saturday, Allie and I would sleep in. And when we woke up, my mother would be preparing the "breakfast of life." You know what that is: grits, with butter; scrambled eggs with onions (sometimes she'd mix up some ground beef in them); fresh-baked biscuits with her own homemade preserves spread all over those; fresh-squeezed orange juice. . . . Ooooh! The "breakfast of life"!

And while we waited for this feast *(she sits on the floor)*, Allie and I would watch cartoons! *(Singing, arms outstretched, as if flying:)*

> "Here I come to save the day!
> That means that Mighty Mouse is on the way!"

One Saturday, just after "Mighty Mouse" went off, Mommy came into the living room and said, "Charlayne, we've run out of grits. Run up to Bernie's corner store and get me a box."

(Pause.)

I looked around and Allie had totally disappeared.

Then my mother said, "Charlayne, it's raining out. You can wear your new rain slicker."

(She stands.)

My new yellow rain slicker! I had been waiting for two weeks to wear my new yellow rain slicker. I got dressed in a flash, and Mommy took that rain slicker out of the closet. I put it on. You could still smell the rubber! It was too big for me, so Mommy had to roll up the sleeves, so I had two huge cuffs right at my wrists. And it had this really *keen* hood that would just grip your face. *(She demonstrates with her hands.)* You couldn't see from side to side. And then it had this really *keen* beak that came down like this, so when the rain hit, the water would just slide off your head! Whoosh!

Mommy gave me a dollar. I tell you, I couldn't wait to get out into that rain!

But when I got outside, there was just . . . a slight drizzle.

Luckily, there were these really great puddles left over from last night's downpour.

(She jumps from puddle to puddle.)

Made it to Bernie's.

"Good morning, Bernie. Look at me! Can I have a box of grits, please? *(Listens to Bernie.)* A licorice?! Sure. Thanks, Bernie. . . . Oh, Bernie, can I have one for Allie, please . . . ? Thank you, Bernie."

Bernie passed me the grits in a brown paper bag, and he gave me my change.

When I looked outside, it was pouring rain. I couldn't wait to get out in it.

(Singing and dancing à la Gene Kelly:)

"White choral bells,
Upon a slender stalk,
Lilies of the valley,
Deck my garden walk—"

"Hey, Bonesy . . . !"

(She freezes.)

Robert Blair. I couldn't see him. But I could feel him right in back of me. So I started walking really fast down Second Street in that rain. Then he came right up beside me. He was so close he was touching my arm. I couldn't see him, though, because of my keen hood.

"Hey, Bonesy . . . when you gonna give me some?"

(Puzzled:) And I'm thinking . . . "Gimme some *what*?"

Then I just took off, running . . . running down Second Street, as fast as I could, in that rain. But Robert Blair was one of those big boys. And he was doing what big boys do.

He ran in front of me, backpedaling, blocking me. . . . I couldn't get around him. But then I saw School 6 just ahead and I knew there was a lot of room there, so if I ran as fast as I possibly could, I could get around Robert Blair. But when I tried . . . he grabbed me, he pushed me up, up, up onto School 6's steps, up against the iron gates that locked the school. He snatched my hood down off my head. He wrapped his arm around that iron bar in back of my head and grabbed my hair. He took his other hand and he held me at my throat.

(Pause.)

No one was out in that rain that day. No one in the whole world, but me . . . and Robert Blair.

He was pressing up against me. He was breathing on me. And I watched a drop of rain slide down his nose and onto my rain slicker.

(Pause.)

"Let me go, Robert Blair. Please?"

He knocked the grits out of my arm, onto the stone steps.

And still pressing up against me, he took his hand and put it . . . up under my rain slicker, and he placed it . . . in between my legs.

(Pause.)

"Please let me go, Robert Blair."

"What do you call this . . . Bonesy?"

"I don't know what you call it. I don't call it anything. Honest."

And then he *squeezed* me down there, really hard.

"You got to call it something, Bonesy! I said what do you call it?"

(In pain, frightened:) "I don't know what you call it, Robert Blair. Honest to God. I don't call it anything."

(Banging her head into the iron bars for emphasis as he speaks:) "What . . . do . . . you . . . call . . . this, Bonesy?"

(Searching desperately for an answer:) "Okay . . . okay . . . okay . . . my mother's a nurse . . . she calls it something. *(He squeezes her down there.)* My mother . . . calls it . . . it's . . . Okay . . . ! Okay . . . ! It's . . . a ragina . . . ?"

(Pause.)

"A what?"

(Yelling desperately:) "It's a ragina!"

"What the hell is a 'ragina,' Bonesy? Don't give me any of your big words! *(He squeezes her.)* I said *(banging her head again)*, what do you call this?!"

"Okay . . . okay . . . wait . . . wait . . . I have a cousin, a little cousin, she's three years old, *she* calls it something. *(Still searching desperately:)* It's a . . . it's . . . it's . . . *(humiliated)* a pee-pee hole?"

(Pause.)

Well, the light came to Robert Blair's face. I watched him . . . throw back his head, and fall back into that rain. *(He laughs grotesquely, his arms outstretched in victory, swooping and soaring all over the stage, yelling at the top of his lungs.)* "It's a pee-pee hole! It's a pee-pee hole!"

Just like some horrible bird, Robert Blair *flew* all the way up Second Street. Laughing at me!

(She notices what's left of the grits on the stone steps. Defeated, she kneels and attempts to gather as much as she can, and puts it back into the soaked box. Painfully, she stands and walks to her house. She's about to knock on the door,

when she stops and decides to wipe away her tears. She pulls her "keen" hood back on her head, then . . . she knocks on the door.)

"I'm sorry, Mommy. I dropped the grits."

"Would you look at you. You certainly did get caught in that downpour. Oh, it's okay, Charlayne. It's just a box of grits. Give me this mess." *(Mother takes the wet, tattered box and throws it out.)*

Then Mommy went into her bedroom and she came back with a dollar and an umbrella. "Here. Run back to Bernie's and get me another box. Hurry now. Breakfast is waiting."

And I just lost my legs and fell to the rug. I couldn't stand anymore.

"Charlayne, hey, come on. It's okay. *(She kisses her.)* It's okay. You don't have to go back. . . . No . . . Come on, let's get you out of these wet clothes. *(Mommy helps her out of her rain slicker, shakes the water off, and hangs it up on a hook.)* Take off those shoes and socks. I know your feet are soaked."

Then my mother put on her own raincoat. She took back the dollar and the umbrella. "I'm sorry. I know. I should've gone myself in the first place. I only sent you because I thought you liked . . . walking in the rain."

And she left.

(Pause.)

I could hear Daddy puttering around in the basement, but I couldn't find Allie anywhere. And then I did. She was in her new hiding place, up under the dining room table, stretched out on the seats of the chairs. She was peeking out at me from underneath the lace tablecloth. And I could tell

. . . by the look in my sister's eyes . . . that Allie already knew all too well . . . what had happened to me.

(Pause.)

We never talked about it.

(Pause.)

So . . . now . . . who has a secret to share with me?

Blackout.

JOY

A shaft of light comes up slowly on CHARLAYNE *as she sings:*

"Have you anything to give
To the Master? Ooh, ooh, ooh.
Have you offered your blessings
To the Lord? Ooh, ooh."

What makes a little girl want to grow up to be a performing artist?

For me, it all started with a dying wish.

(Lights up.)

Way back in 1927, in Shibuta, Mississippi, my grandparents—Daddy's parents, Alfred Sr. and Leola—along with their brothers and sisters, took their life savings, plus the savings of *generations* of Woodards and McCanns before them, and with the help of a white intermediary, they bought one hundred acres of prime, beautiful farmland in upstate New York, five miles outside of Albany. My grandmother likes to say *(as Grandmama, with a soft, sweet, rural accent),*

"God *delivered* us . . . from out of Shibuta, Mississippi . . . and brought us to . . . the promised land."

*(*CHARLAYNE *sings:)*

"My father is rich,
In houses and land.
He holdeth the power of the world,
In his hands. . . ."

My grandparents lived a "saved, sanctified, filled-with-the-Holy Ghost" kind of existence since they were children. Everything they knew, they shared with us. They taught us all about love, life, tolerance, charity . . . berry picking. . . .

When the women's lib movement came about, we were all very anxious to hear Grandmama's views on *that* subject. She gathered her granddaughters around her. She said *(as Grandmama)*, "Generations and generations of Woodard women . . . have always had . . . the opportunity . . . to work like a man, and at a man's job. Oh, we have all worked in the fields, chopped wood, driven trucks, and tractors, and buses. I myself, I worked on the railroad during the war. A woman must always be prepared to do whatever she has to do, for the sake of her family and her loved ones. . . . But if any of you should find a nice young man . . . he comes walking down the street, and this young man just happens to be offering you . . . a pedestal . . . I want you to climb up on it, and take a nap for me!"

*(*CHARLAYNE *sings:)*

"I've got joy like a river,
That the Lord God gave to me."

By the time I was eleven years old, Grandmama had eight children, twenty grands. Every Sunday after church, we'd all gather at Grandmama's house for the big Sunday dinner.

One such Sunday, Grandmama said, "Lord . . . before I die . . . I sure would love to hear one of my grands . . . sing with that Wilborn's Temple Church of God in Christ Junior Church Choir."

And we thought, "Oh my goodness! This is important. Grandmama's about to die. This is her dying wish."

Now, at the time, Grandmama had five grandchildren who qualified for the Wilborn's Temple Church of God in Christ Junior Church Choir: me and Allie, my cousins Mary and Lois, and my cousin Freddie.

We were all very anxious to make Grandmama's dying wish come true, so we found out that the Junior Church Choir met at six-thirty on Wednesday evenings. That very next Wednesday, we joined the Wilborn's Temple Church of God in Christ Junior Church Choir.

After three Wednesday rehearsals, it was Junior Church Sunday. The Junior Church Choir would be singing all day long, morning service and evening service.

(She moves loveseat upstage right.)

We five cousins waited excitedly, with the rest of the choir, at the back of the church, behind two huge double doors. There were forty-three of us—forty girls, three boys. We were all in black and white. The boys wore black suits, white shirts, black bow ties. The girls wore black circle skirts and white starched blouses with big wide bows tied at the neck. Grandmama's granddaughters wore black velvet circle skirts that she had made herself, specially for us.

Loren Cade, our choir director, arranged us in a line according to height, the shortest in the front.

Oh! A word about Loren Cade. Loren Cade was one of those people who was so fabulous, you had to call him by both names at all times . . . Loren Cade. We all secretly had a mad crush on Loren Cade, and we just *loved* it when he would touch us, ever so slightly, to put us in line. Oh . . . but it was hopeless. Nothing could ever come of it. You see, Loren Cade was a grown-up. . . . He was seventeen!

We stood in the back of the church. The music started up at the front of the church. My uncle Willie, the assistant pastor, came into the pulpit and asked the congregation to "please rise" on both sides of that center aisle.

Loren Cade stood in front of us all, and he opened up those big double doors, and we came marching down that aisle.

(She sings and marches:)

"We are marchin',
Up freedom's highway,
We are marchin',
Each and every day. . . ."

I couldn't *see* her, because she was way up in front, in the "mothers'" section, oh, but I could *hear* her. . . . *My grandmother*—from the moment we came through those big double doors—stood to her feet . . . *(as Grandmama, with absolute joy:)* "Hallelujah! Glory, glory, glory! Praises to God!"

*(*CHARLAYNE *continues down the aisle, singing and marching.)*

"Made up my mind,
And I won't turn back,
Made up my mind,
And I won't turn back. . . ."

(She sits on the loveseat, which is now the choir stand.)

We slid into the choir stand. Us five cousins tried desperately to catch Grandmama's eye. But she wouldn't give it to us. She just sat there, directly across the church from the choir stand, in the "mothers' " section, all dressed in white, beaming with satisfaction. *(She beams.)*

(Standing:) The choir sang an 'A' and 'B' selection.

Then Sister Hattie Tanksley came to the microphone to deliver the announcements of the week. After that, it was time for the bishop to come into the pulpit and deliver the Word. As far as we were concerned, that meant it was time for us to go digging into our little black patent-leather pocketbooks. We'd trade Life Savers for Good and Plentys and Good and Plentys for Jujubes . . . and pass notes about Loren Cade. . . . Then, in the middle of the sermon, from way across the church in the "mothers' " section, Mother Wilborn would haul off and say *(becoming Mother Wilborn)*, "Ssssh! *(Pointing her finger:)* Come on now!" And I'd just pray Mommy didn't see that. . . .

Finally, the Word was over, and we all stood for the benediction.

(She sings:)

> "Thank you, Lord,
> Thank you, Lord,
> Thank you, Lord.
> I just want to thank you, Lord."

As we bowed our heads for the benediction, something told me to . . . look up. And she winked at me!

When church was over, we five cousins stood there and watched Grandmama walk down that center aisle with her cane. She had her head held high as she walked straight through those big double doors. . . .

(As they watch Grandmama exit:) Allie asked, "Is Grandmama gonna die now?"

"I don't know, Allie, but if she does, she'll die happy."

Several Sundays passed, and again we were out at Grandmama's for that wonderful Sunday dinner. This time she was standing at the stove, frying some chicken, when she just hauled off and said, "Lord . . . before I die . . . I sure would love to hear one of my grands sing . . . a solo . . . with that Wilborn's Temple Church of God in Christ Junior Church Choir."

Now, how could Grandmama stand there at that stove, on a Sunday afternoon, frying up chicken, and come up with a *second* dying wish? This was way out of our control! I mean, there's courage in numbers. We could sing *with* the choir all day long. But . . . a *solo?*

My cousin Freddie just raised his hand and said, "Grandmama, Grandmama! I'm just too young!"

My cousins Mary and Lois stood there very willing, but very tone deaf. My sister, Allie, just crossed her legs and went running off to the bathroom. . . . You know you can't put Allie under any pressure!

So that left me.

The very next Wednesday night, at the end of choir rehearsal, when all the other kids were in the back of the church waiting for our parents to come pick us up, I approached Marguerite Johnson. Marguerite Johnson was the head of the whole Junior Church Choir. Even over Loren Cade.

(Unsure of herself:) "Marguerite, can I have a song?"

Marguerite just looked at me. You see, you didn't have to audition to get into the Wilborn's Temple Church of God in

Christ Junior Church Choir, but if you wanted . . . a solo, you had to have been in that choir for at least six or seven months.

Marguerite said, "Charlayne Woodard, I don't even know your voice. Come on over to the piano. I'm going to play some scales and I want you to repeat them after me. Here we go . . . *(Marguerite plays a scale, singing:)* La, la, la, la, la, la, la, la, la."

*(*CHARLAYNE, *with great trepidation:)* "La, la, la, la . . . la, la . . . la, la. . . ."

"Come on now, baby. I need you to breathe. Breathe and support it. Breathe now. *(*MARGUERITE *plays a higher scale:)* La, la, la, la, la, la, la, la."

*(*CHARLAYNE *takes several very deep breaths, then belts the scale, with no control:)* "La, la, la, la, la, la, la, la!"

(Pause.)

Marguerite walked over to her box of records and she picked one out. "The first song on the first side. If you can learn it . . . we'll see."

I took this record home, I listened to that song, and I learned that song. The very next Tuesday, I called Marguerite and told her, "Marguerite, I know my song."

She said, "Very good, we'll rehearse it tomorrow."

That night, when I took my bath, I noticed that my whole back had broken out into a mountain of bumps! I was so afraid of singing in front of those forty-two kids.

The next night, at choir rehearsal, the whole choir was *(crossing stage)* over here learning their section of the song, and I was *(crossing back)* way over here singing my section . . . sotto voce. Marguerite came over and put her ear to my mouth to see if I was truly singing. But I was truly singing . . . only sotto voce.

Then my sister, Allie, yells out, "Come on, Charlayne, we can't even hear you!"

I said, "Oh, shut up, Allie!"

Finally, choir rehearsal was over and I'd gotten away with it!

So about three Wednesday rehearsals went by, and again it was Junior Church Sunday. The Junior Church Choir was singing all day long, morning service and evening service. We lined up in back of the church, the music started up in the front, and Uncle Willie asked the congregation to rise. Loren Cade opened up those big double doors, and we came marching through, with a *new* song and a *new* step.

(She sings and marches:)

"Climbing up the mountain,
Trying to reach the top,
Climbing Jacob's ladder,
Climb, climb, climbing,
And I just can't stop.
And at the end of the mountain,
There is faith and trust,
I can see Jesus,
Waiting for us.
And I thank God,
I'm reaching for my soul."

We slid into the choir stand! *(She sits.)* We five cousins tried desperately to catch Grandmama's eye, but she still wouldn't give it to us. She just sat there, in the "mothers' " section, beaming, beaming, beaming!

(Standing:) We gave an 'A' and 'B' selection, and then *(walking across the stage as the very proper, very haughty Sister Hattie Tanksley)* Sister Hattie Tanksley came to the mi-

crophone to deliver the announcements of the week. *(Tapping the mike:)* "Test . . . test . . . test . . . *(She clears her throat.)* In the dining room this afternoon, we are serving fried chicken dinners, with er, a . . . collard greens, and er, a . . . corn bread, and er, a . . . chitterlings. . . ."

While Sister Hattie Tanksley was going on and on with the menu, I noticed Marguerite Johnson trying to get Loren Cade's attention. And when she did, she pointed at me. Allie was sitting right in back of me and she saw all of this going on. She started scratching at the back of my neck. "Charlayne, Charlayne! *Your* song is next! *Your* song is next!"

And I said, "I know it, Allie! Stop it!"

(Pause.)

My heart was in my neck. And I just kept praying that Sister Hattie Tanksley would never end that menu. Oh, but she did. Sister Hattie Tanksley sat down, and Loren Cade stood up. . . . In front of the whole congregation, he gave the signal for the choir to rise to its feet. *(She stands.)* He pointed to me . . . and then he pointed to that mike.

(Pause.)

(Sidestepping:) No sooner did she see me start sidestepping through the choir stand, my grandmother . . . stood to her feet. *(With absolute joy:)* "Hallelujah! Glory! Glory! Glory! Praises to God!"

The sheer *power* of her faith ignited the congregation that day. By the time I reached the microphone, the saints were up on their feet, praising God, glorifying His name, calling on the Lord!

I stood there. The microphone towered over my head.

Loren Cade came over . . . and lowered it . . . to my mouth.

The music started up. Loren Cade put us in a sway. *(She steps from side to side.)*

I looked over at Grandmama . . . and fear . . . *flew* from me.

(Completely focused on Grandmama, singing with all her heart:)

"God . . . gave me a song,
That the angels cannot sing,
I've been washed in the blood. . . ."

Well, the church went up! The Spirit ran through! The people were up on their feet, dancing and praising God! Sister Geneva Conway wrapped her skirt around her legs and ran . . . up and down the center aisle! And my very own grandmother . . . walked around her cane! *(Grandmama walks around her cane in celebration.)* "Hallelujah! Glory, glory, glory! Praises to God!"

And we sang on and on. We couldn't stop singing. Something *wonderful* was happening that day. Loren Cade just kept giving the signal *(rolling his fists in a circle):* "Repeat! Repeat! Repeat! Repeat!" And we kept singing! We just kept singing!

Finally, my uncle Willie came into the pulpit. *(Arms outstretched:)* "All right now, it's time for the Word! Come on . . . yes . . . it's time. Time for the Word. Yes . . . time for the Word. . . . Hallelujah!"

(Pause.)

Loren Cade signaled me to return to my seat *(sidestepping back)* and he gave us the signal to sit. *(She sits.)* I tell you, I was shaking all over. The whole choir, we were shaking all over. We were stunned. That had never happened before.

Never had the Spirit run through that congregation like that . . . never did the saints shout and praise God like that—never! Not when the Wilborn's Temple Church of God in Christ *Junior* Church Choir sang!

When the bishop stood in the pulpit to deliver the Word *(awed)*, we just sat there. Nobody went digging in her pocketbook. Nobody traded Good and Plentys for Jujubes. Nobody even passed notes about Loren Cade. We just sat there . . . and *listened* to the Word.

When the sermon was over, we all stood for the benediction. *(She stands.)*

When church was over, all the parents and relatives came and mobbed the choir stand, hugging and praising all the kids. *(She sits.)* And I just sat there . . . *waiting* . . . for her. I knew she was there when I could smell . . . vanilla.

(She stands slowly, looking up at her grandmother.)

She . . . wrapped her arms around me.

(Grandmama sings:)

"Oh, what a pretty little baby,
A pretty little baby,
Born in a manger,
Oh what a pretty little baby,
Jesus is his name."

(Time seems to stand still as CHARLAYNE *and Grandmama share a silent moment, in which Grandmama says, "I'm proud of you," and* CHARLAYNE *answers, "Thank you, Grandmama.")*

. . . And we watched Grandmama . . . walk down that center aisle . . . straight through those big double doors.

(Pause.)

The next morning, I came barreling into the kitchen. My mother was standing at the stove, cooking oatmeal.

(Victorious:) "Mommy, was that *me*? Was that *me* who set that church on fire? Was that me who had those saints shouting and dancing in the aisles? *(She imitates a holy dance.)* Was it me, Mommy, who had those grown-ups *in the palm of my hand*?"

My mother just stood there . . . stirring up oatmeal. She said . . . "No . . . that was not you. That was *God.* That was the Spirit of the Lord, Charlayne, using you, working through you, to bless that congregation yesterday. No, no, no, little missy, that was not you . . . that was God. And don't you ever forget it."

(Deflated:) Now, I must admit I thought it an honor and a privilege to be used by God like that, but deep in my heart I was truly disappointed. *I* wanted to be the one with all that power. I wanted it to be *me* that had those saints shouting like that. And most of all . . . I wanted Mommy to be proud of me.

But my mother just came over to the table. She handed Allie her bowl of oatmeal, and she handed me mine. . . . *(She looks back and forth between the bowls and then up at her mother, and then to the audience; she says simply:)* Mine had raisins in it! *(She beams.)*

(Pause.)

(She sings:)

"I want to live,
So God can use me,
Anytime and anywhere."

Ever since that Sunday, I've been on stages all over the world, sharing God's gifts, and all the while marveling. And all because of a dying wish . . . or two.

Oh . . . about that dying wish. My grandmother . . . Leola Woodard . . . just died . . . October 21st, 1991.

(Miles Davis's "All Blues" plays softly.)

Thank you, Grandmama. Thank you, God. Thank you, ladies and gentlemen.

Blackout.

CURTAIN